# Penguin's Hidden Talent

by Alex Latimer

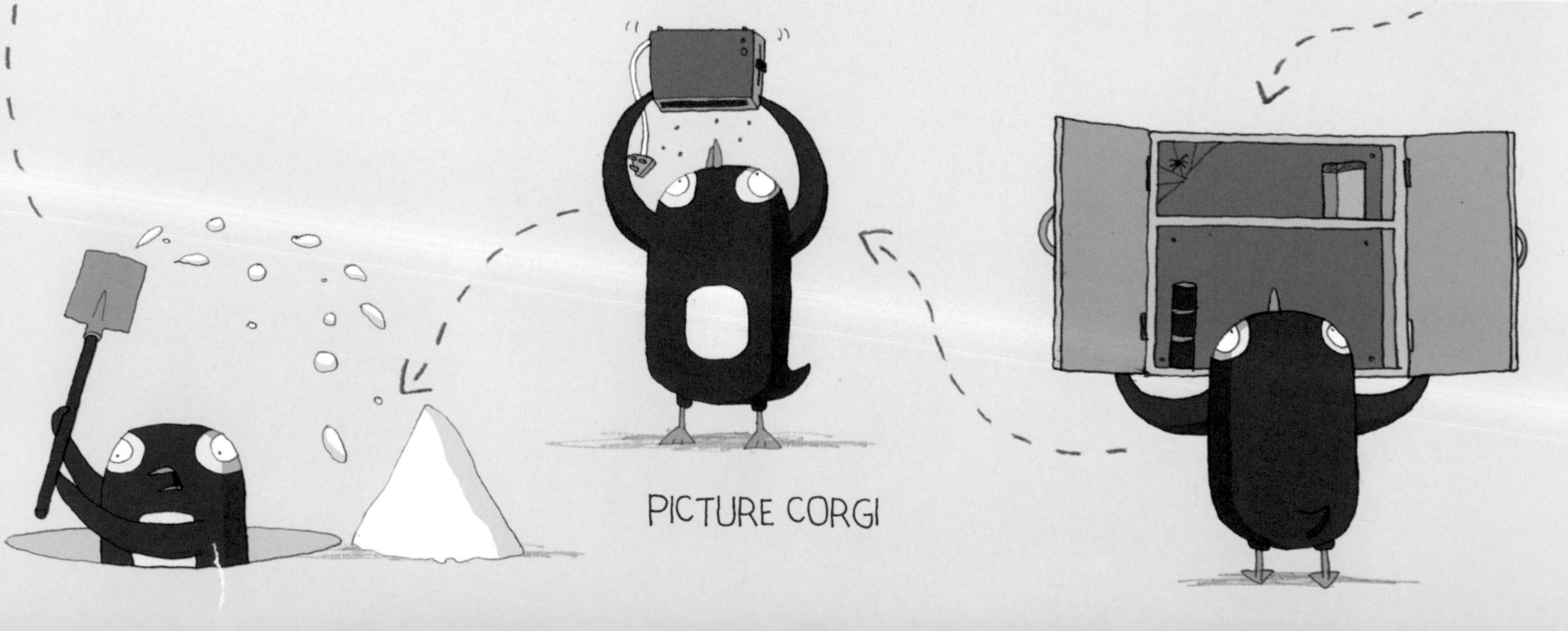

PICTURE CORGI

for Lily

Penguin's Hidden Talent
A PICTURE CORGI BOOK
978 0 552 573 016 First published in
Great Britain by Picture Corgi, an imprint
of Random House Children's Books A Random House
Group Company This edition published 2012
1 3 5 7 9 10 8 6 4 2

Picture Corgi Books are published by Random House
Children's Books, 61-63 Uxbridge Road, London W5 5SA
www.kidsatrandomhouse.co.uk
www.randomhouse.co.uk
Addresses for companies within
The Random House Group Limited
can be found at:
www.randomhouse.
co.uk/offices.htm
THE RANDOM HOUSE GROUP
Limited Reg. No. 954009
A CIP catalogue record for
this book is available
from the British Library.
Printed and bound
in China.

The BIG annual Talent Show was
just round the corner. . .

. . .and everyone was practising.

Ta-da!

Everyone except Penguin.
Penguin couldn't think what his talent was.

It wasn't baking.

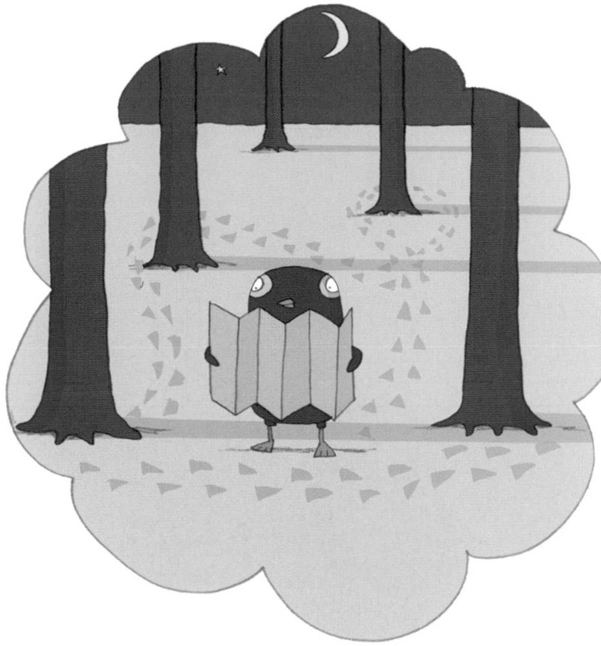

It wasn't map reading.

And it wasn't knitting.

Albatross wanted to help Penguin find his talent.
"Have you ever tried swallowing a whole marlin?" he asked.

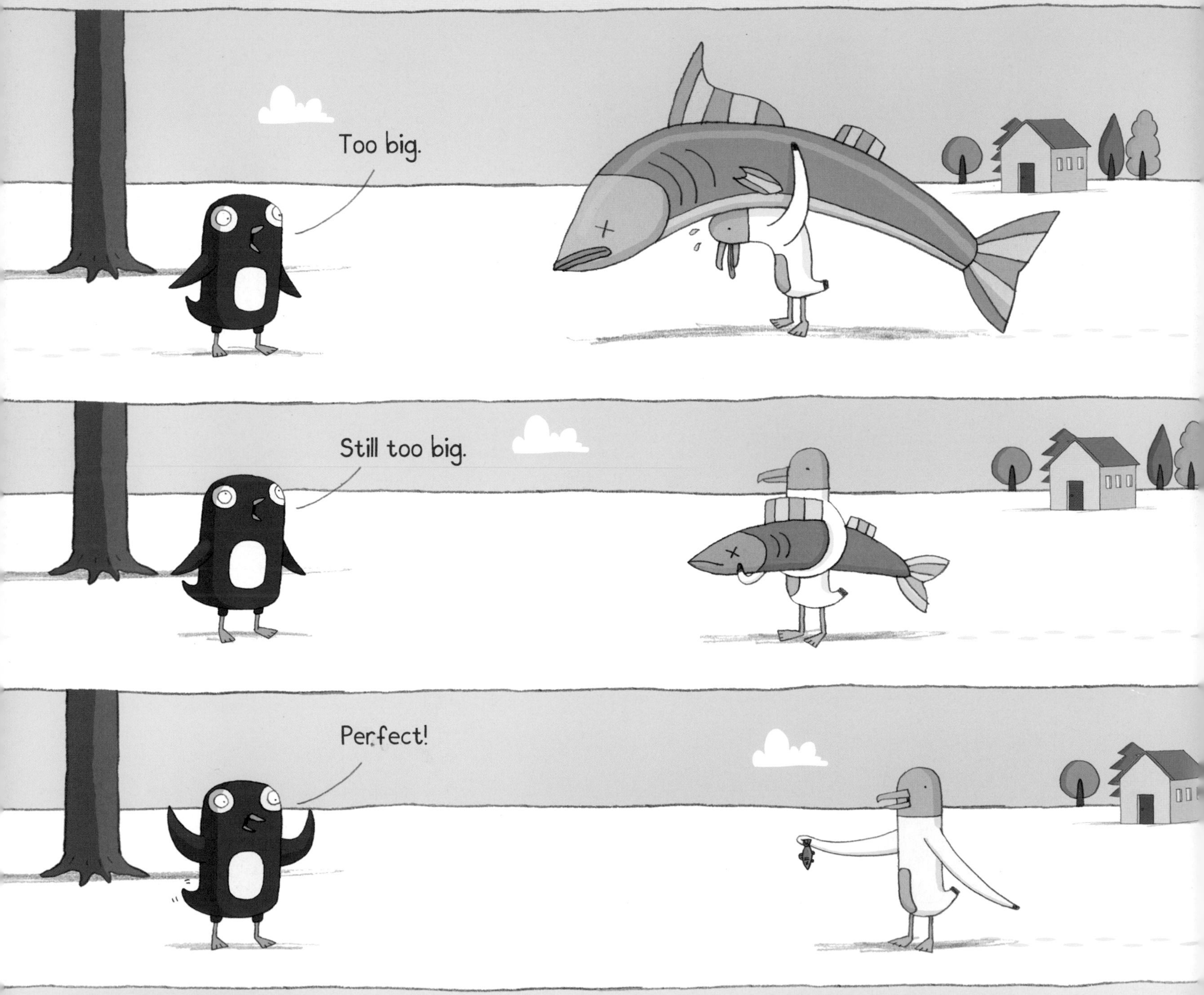


But Penguin could only swallow a sardine.

Bear also wanted to help.
"Have you ever tried
juggling appliances?"
he asked.

But Penguin only managed to break a blender
and get a toaster stuck up a tree.

"Have you tried doing magic tricks?" asked Rabbit.
But though Penguin made Rabbit's watch disappear. . .

he couldn't bring it back again.

"Have you tried burping the alphabet?" asked Fox.

ABCDEFGHIJKL

But all Penguin could
do was hiccup.

hiccup

"Don't worry about me," said Penguin. "I'll just help organise the Talent Show. That way I can still be involved, even though I don't have a talent."

So while his friends practised
Penguin drew posters,

made phone calls,

sent emails,

and polished the trophy.

Finally the big day arrived.

The opening ceremony was terrific.

There were fireworks, and jets,
and loads of good music.

Then a guest speaker spoke.
crust
sugar
stewed apples
lemon juice & spices
You have to believe in yourself. . .
Is that the King of Norway?
Ooh, yes. I believe it is.

And a famous band played.

Then the show started.

Albatross, Fox, Bear and Rabbit all did exceptionally well.

kazam

The judges took ages to count up the points, but eventually they came to a decision.

"The winner of this year's Talent Show is. . .
BEAR!

With medals of excellence going to
Albatross, Fox and Rabbit!"

Everyone celebrated.
But not Penguin.
After all, he didn't have a medal.

And he walked slowly home through the snow.

Bear, Albatross, Fox and Rabbit were very worried about Penguin. They tried to think of a way to cheer him up.

"I know," said Rabbit.
"Let's throw Penguin a party
to thank him for organising
the Talent Show!"

Everyone agreed that
it was a very good idea.

And they all
worked late
into the night
to organise a
great party.

The next morning, when Penguin came outside for the newspaper, he found that his friends had thrown him a party. And it wasn't a very good one.

Albatross had made a tatty banner
that said, THAKS PEMGIN.
The only music that Rabbit could organise
was a singing canary.
Fox brought his gran as the guest speaker.
And Bear brought an old loaf of bread
instead of a cake.

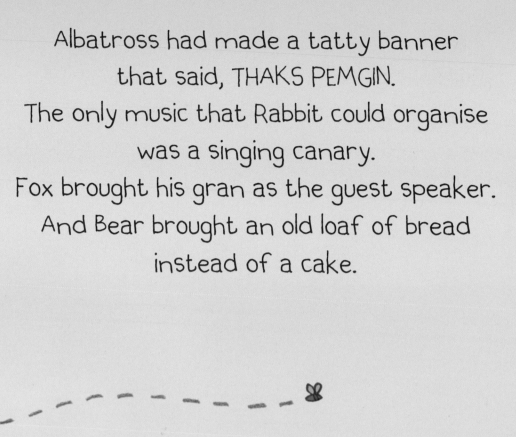

And I'll tell you another thing about sandwiches. . .

"If only you'd organised this party, Penguin," said Rabbit. "Then it wouldn't be so terrible."

And just then, Penguin realised how talented he really was.

I don't need a medal.
I need a telephone.

Hello. I'd like to order. . .

ice cream
What a great party!

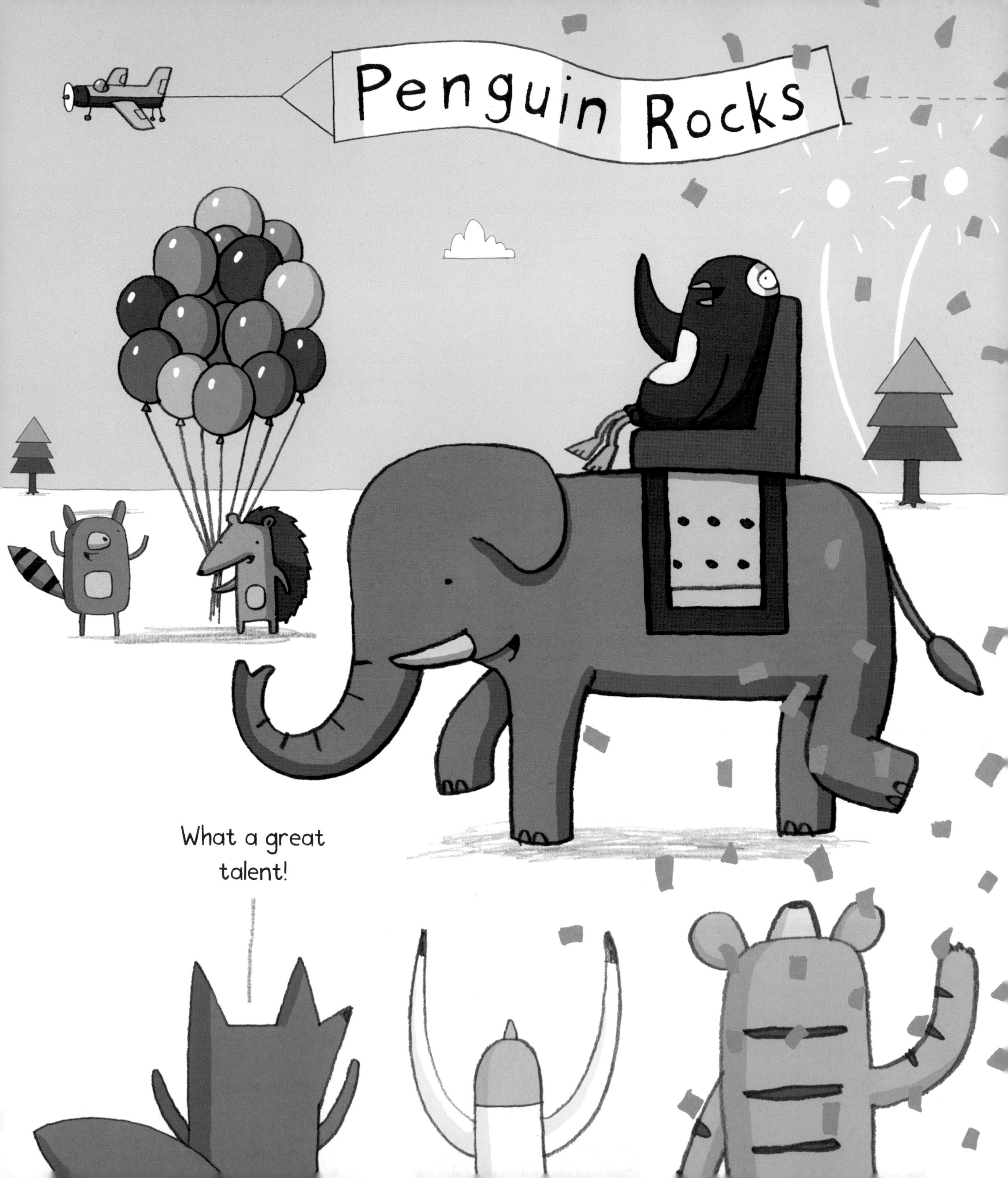
Penguin Rocks
What a great talent!

PENGUIN
PARTY PLANNER
CALL: LOUDLY